There's an Alien

IN YOUR BOOK

Written by TOM FLETCHER

Illustrated by GREG ABBOTT

Random House 🏠 New York

For Max —T.F.

For Annika —G.A.

Copyright © 2020 by Tom Fletcher
Illustrated by Greg Abbott

All rights reserved. Published in the United States by Random House Children's Books,
a division of Penguin Random House LLC, New York. Originally published by Puffin Books,
an imprint of Penguin Random House Children's Books U.K., a division of Penguin Random House U.K., London, in 2019.

Random House and the colophon are registered trademarks of Penguin Random House LLC.

Visit us on the Web! rhcbooks.com

Educators and librarians, for a variety of teaching tools, visit us at RHTeachersLibrarians.com

Library of Congress Cataloging-in-Publication Data
Names: Fletcher, Tom, author. | Abbott, Greg, illustrator.
Title: There's an alien in your book / written by Tom Fletcher ; illustrated by Greg Abbott.
Other titles: There is an alien in your book
Description: First American edition. | New York : Random House Children's Books, [2020] |
"Originally published by Puffin Books, an imprint of Penguin Random House Children's Books U.K.,
a division of Penguin Random House U.K., London, in 2019" | Audience: Ages 3–7. | Audience: Grades K–1. |
Summary: Encourages the reader to shake, tilt, and wiggle the book in an effort to launch
the alien back into space, because aliens do not belong on Earth—or maybe they do.
Identifiers: LCCN 2019030483 (print) | LCCN 2019030484 (ebook) |
ISBN 978-0-593-12512-0 (hardcover) | ISBN 978-0-593-12513-7 (ebook)
Subjects: LCSH: Extraterrestrial beings—Juvenile fiction. | Books—Juvenile fiction. | Friendship—Juvenile fiction. |
Humorous stories. | CYAC: Extraterrestrial beings—Fiction. | Books—Fiction. | Friendship—Fiction. |
Humorous stories. | LCGFT: Humorous fiction. Classification: LCC PZ7.F6358 Thj 2020 (print) |
LCC PZ7.F6358 (ebook) |
DDC 823.92 [E]—dc23

MANUFACTURED IN CHINA
10 9 8 7 6 5 4 3 2 1
First American Edition

OH NO!
A spaceship has crash-landed in your book!

What a lot of smoke!
    I think something is there. . . .

Blow the smoke away
and turn the page. . . .

AAAARGH! It's an ALIEN!

Look at that big, round head . . . yuck!

And those wibbly-wobbly antennae . . . double yuck!

And all those slimy suckers . . .
yuck, yuck, **Yuck!**

Make your scariest face and shout . . .
Go away, Alien!

OH NO!

It's crying.
Perhaps we shouldn't have been so mean.

Pat the alien's head to make it feel better.

That's better—look, it's smiling!
(I don't know what it's saying, though—do you?)

Now we need to help Alien get back
up into space. But . . .

We'll have to find another way.

JIGGLE the book UP and DOWN—
that might bounce it back into space. . . .

Wow! You bounced Alien high,
but not high enough.

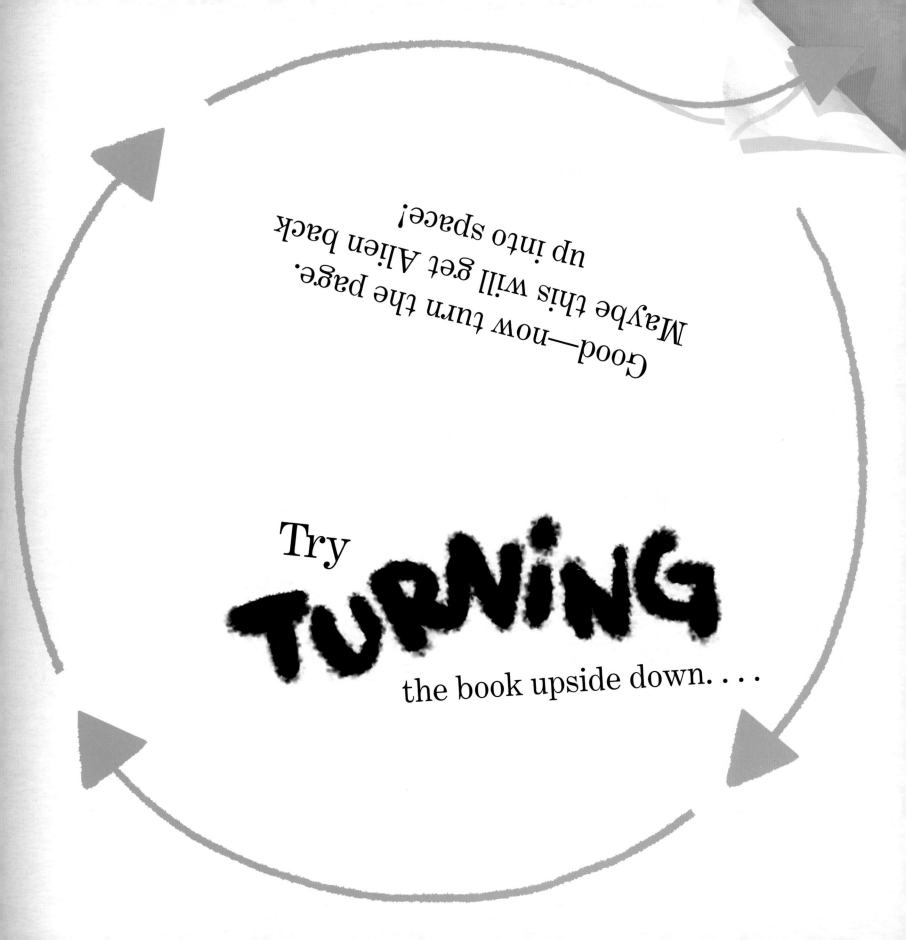

Try **TURNING** the book upside down. . . .

Good—now turn the page. Maybe this will get Alien back up into space!

Look! Alien is standing on its head—
but it's not in space!

Try LIFTING the book HIGH up
in the air and turn the page. . . .

UH-OH!

Alien is very high up,
but it's STILL not in space—
and it looks a little scared!

Phew!

Alien is safe
back on the
ground.

But aliens don't belong on Earth—
they're much too different.

Earth is for people . . . and pugs . . .
frogs and bugs,
fish and snails,
bees and whales—right?

Close your eyes and IMAGINE these creatures.

Hang on—
all those things look pretty different too!

Alien, you've got googly eyes,
wibbly-wobbly antennae,
and skin slimier than a slug, but . . .

we're all weird and wonderful. . . .

So you're welcome to stay here on Planet Earth!

Now, if Alien is going to stay,
I think it needs a home in this book.

Use your finger to draw a house shape here,
then close your eyes, say **zaa-zee-zoo**,
and turn the page. . . .

That looks like the

perfect

home!

Hmm—I think Alien needs a friend to play with.

Shout ...

Come and be friends with Alien!
as loudly as you can.

Well done! It worked!
You called a friendly little monster.

I think he'll make a great friend for Alien—
don't you?

And Monster has a surprise for Alien. . . .

He's fixed the spaceship!
Now they're ready for an . . .

adventure!

Press the button on the spaceship and count down—5, 4, 3, 2, 1 . . .

LIFTOFF!
Wave goodbye to Alien and Monster, and say . . .

zaa-zee-zoo!